Andrew Sharmat

SMEDGE

pictures by
Chris L. Demarest

Macmillan Publishing Company   New York
Collier Macmillan Publishers   London

To my parents...
for all your love and encouragement
—A.S.

For Alison and Foobie
—C.D.

Text copyright © 1989 by Andrew Sharmat
Illustrations copyright © 1989 by Chris L. Demarest
All rights reserved. No part of this book may be reproduced or
transmitted in any form or by any means, electronic or mechanical,
including photocopying, recording, or by any information storage and
retrieval system, without permission in writing from the Publisher.
Macmillan Publishing Company
866 Third Avenue, New York, NY 10022
Collier Macmillan Canada, Inc.
Printed and bound in Singapore
First American Edition

10 9 8 7 6 5 4 3 2 1

The text of this book is set in 16 point Garamond No. 3.
The illustrations are rendered in watercolor and pen-and-ink.
Library of Congress Cataloging-in-Publication Data
Sharmat, Andrew.
Smedge.
Summary: Mr. and Mrs. Pettey's dog Smedge leads a double
life as an important diplomat in Washington, D.C., where
he makes headlines by biting a queen at a dinner party.
[1. Dogs—Fiction. 2. Humorous stories]
I. Demarest, Chris L., ill. II. Title.
PZ7.S52988Sm 1989 [E] 88-13733
ISBN 0-02-782261-3

Mr. and Mrs. Pettey and their dog, Smedge,
lived in a small house in the small town of
Sparrow's Corners. Each morning, at exactly
eight o'clock, Mr. and Mrs. Pettey drove off to
work at a small factory, and each evening, at
exactly six o'clock, they returned home.

For many years the Pettey family lived this way and thought themselves very happy. But one morning Mrs. Pettey realized that not everyone in the family was happy.

"Do you think Smedge is bored?" she asked Mr. Pettey. "He sleeps all the time and he hardly touches his food. He's been this way ever since his birthday two years ago. Remember his birthday party? It was so much fun! And those lovely gifts we gave him—a vested suit and a briefcase."

"You know, maybe those gifts were a little strange for a dog," replied Mr. Pettey.

Before Mrs. Pettey could answer, the Petteys'
grandfather clock struck eight. Mr. and Mrs.
Pettey each gave Smedge a big hug and drove
off to work.

As soon as they left, Smedge got up out of his corner, put on his suit, grabbed his briefcase,

and caught the 8:15 train to Washington, D.C.

When he arrived in Washington, Smedge's limousine was waiting for him.

"Good morning, Mr. S. Winston Scott," said the driver. "You're looking fine, as always." He opened the door for Smedge, waited until Smedge was seated inside, and then closed the door.

When Smedge arrived at his office, his assistants were waiting for him.

"Good morning, Mr. S. Winston Scott," said his assistant. "Here are your papers."

"Good morning, Mr. S. Winston Scott," said the assistant-to-the-assistant. "Here is a list of your meetings for today. Don't forget that you are to have lunch with the Swedish ambassador at twelve o'clock."

"Good morning, Mr. S. Winston Scott," said the assistant-to-the-assistant's-assistant. "Here is your coffee. Cream and sugar. Just the way you like it."

At twelve o'clock, Smedge dined with the Swedish ambassador at Washington's finest restaurant.

At one o'clock he went sailing at the yacht club.

At two o'clock he gave a speech to the
National Hot Dog Association.

At three o'clock he met with the
Vice President of the United States.

Four o'clock found him back in his office for the signing of the treaty ending the Bokastan-Dengli War.

And at five o'clock he was driven to the train station in his limousine. From there he caught the 5:15 train to Sparrow's Corners.

When he returned home, Smedge put away his briefcase, slipped out of his suit, dropped down in the corner of the living room, and closed his eyes.

Exactly three minutes later, a car pulled into the driveway. Mr. and Mrs. Pettey were home.

"Hello, Smedge," said Mr. Pettey, as he and Mrs. Pettey entered the house.

Smedge opened his eyes, stood up, and wagged his tail. Then he slouched down and closed his eyes again.

"Poor Smedge," said Mrs. Pettey. "He looks exhausted."

"Yes," replied Mr. Pettey. "You'd think that he'd just put in a hard day's work at the office."

Smedge opened his eyes a second time, looked at Mr. Pettey, and then closed them again.

"Maybe he'll cheer up if I feed him his dinner," said Mrs. Pettey. She emptied a can of Shepherd's Surprise dog food into Smedge's bowl.

Smedge opened his eyes a third time, looked at Mrs. Pettey, and closed them again.

"You'd think that he'd been eating gourmet food all day," remarked Mr. Pettey.

The next morning when Smedge arrived in
Washington, his limousine was waiting for him
as always.

"Good news, Mr. Scott," his driver said.
"We're going directly to the White House. The
President wants to speak to you."

At the White House, Smedge walked into the Oval Office.

The President stood up. "Mr. Scott," he said, "this afternoon I'm having a very big luncheon for the Queen of Kingwich. As you know, Kingwich is the world's leading maker of pink Ping-Pong balls. At the end of the luncheon the Queen and I will sign an agreement for the United States to buy one million pink Ping-Pong balls. I want you to be there."

That afternoon there were two hundred guests
in the State Dining Room of the White House.
The Queen of Kingwich sat at the head table
with the President of the United States to her
left and Smedge to her right.

The President turned to the Queen. "I would
like you to meet Mr. S. Winston Scott, our
country's chief diplomat."

The Queen gave Smedge a strange look.

Smedge looked back at the Queen.

Just then the waiters brought the soup.

The Queen started to eat her soup. Then she stopped and began staring at Smedge.

At last, she said, "Mr. President, are you aware that your chief diplomat has fleas?"

"Nonsense," said the President.

"And would you please ask your chief diplomat to stop shedding in my soup?"

"My chief diplomat never sheds."

"Well, then, would you be so kind as to tell me why your chief diplomat has very bad breath?"

Smedge started to growl.

The President looked at Smedge. "Mr. Scott," he said, "would you please stop growling at the Queen?"

Smedge growled louder.

"Mr. President, your chief diplomat has very large fangs. I find them quite unattractive."

Smedge sank his teeth into the Queen's arm.

The Queen screamed, "Mr. President, your chief diplomat just bit me! Now I can't sign the pink Ping-Pong ball agreement. The deal is off."

"Mr. Scott, what have you done?" said the President. "You've ruined everything!"

The guards seized Smedge and took him to jail.
He was the only prisoner there who had been
arrested for biting a queen at a luncheon.

Two hours later the President appeared at the jail.

"Mr. Scott," he said, "our spies have just discovered that Kingwich's pink Ping-Pong balls don't bounce. You've saved us from making a terrible mistake! You have performed a wonderful service for your country."

The President got Smedge out of jail.

That night, back in Sparrow's Corners, Mr. and Mrs. Pettey came home from work to find that Smedge wasn't there.

"He's gone!" cried Mr. Pettey.

"Maybe he's just out for a long stroll," replied Mrs. Pettey.

"No, I don't think so," said Mr. Pettey. "His briefcase and vested suit are gone, too. He must have taken them with him."

"I'm so pleased," said Mrs. Pettey. "He really must have liked our gifts after all."

Before supper, Mr. and Mrs. Pettey turned on their television set to watch the news.

"Our major story this evening," said the announcer, "is the awarding of a medal to Mr. S. Winston Scott. Mr. Scott is the first diplomat in history to receive a medal for biting a queen at a luncheon."

"S. Winston Scott?" said Mrs. Pettey. "You know, he looks a little like Smedge, doesn't he? He's even wearing a suit like his."

"Yes," said Mr. Pettey. "He does look like Smedge. I wish Smedge were here to see this. One look at Mr. S. Winston Scott and I bet he would be inspired to do great things, too. Poor Smedge. I wonder where he is."